About the Author

Felicity Scherer is the debut author of the fascinating story *The Dog That Didn't Know How to Cuddle*. Felicity is a busy working mum of two active boys who like to keep her on her toes. Felicity is a children's book lover and is passionate about reading all day, every day to her busy boys. An avid animal lover, she has rescued many pets in her lifetime, and grew up on an action-packed farm. She finds animals an absolute joy, finding their own stories exceptionally captivating. All humans have a story to tell, well guess what, so do animals.

The Dog That Didn't Know How to Cuddle

Felicity Scherer

The Dog That Didn't Know How to Cuddle

Nightingale Books

A CIP catalogue record for this title is
available from the British Library.
ISBN 978-1-83875-616-1

Nightingale Books is an imprint of
Pegasus Elliot MacKenzie Publishers Ltd.
www.pegasuspublishers.com

First Published in 2023

Nightingale Books
Sheraton House Castle Park
Cambridge England

Printed & Bound in Great Britain

Dedication

Liam and Benji, you are my world.

Daisy May Delany thought she was the luckiest dog in the whole wide world. She had the kindest owners, named Betty and Bill, and they loved to spoil Daisy every single day.

Betty and Bill fed Daisy her favourite doggy treats at dinner time and they let her have enormous adventures in the backyard, digging for bones, pulling washing off the line and hiding shoes.

Every day, Betty and Bill took her for big long walks to the park where she sniffed trees and met and played with other friendly dogs.

Daisy was so happy with her wonderful life, but there was one small problem. Daisy May Delany didn't know how to cuddle. Betty and Bill would try and try and try to cuddle Daisy every day. They tried to cuddle her on their fleecy green couch. They tried to cuddle her in their bright red car. They tried to cuddle her on their favourite bright blue blanket. They even tried to cuddle her on their big brass bed. The harder they tried, the more difficult it was to cuddle Daisy.

Daisy wanted, more than anything to cuddle Betty and Bill. However, it was always very uncomfortable for Daisy. It would hurt her little legs and back each time they tried, so Daisy May Delany just gave up trying.

One sunny morning Daisy was scratching in the backyard digging for bones, when she heard a strange purring noise behind her. Daisy turned around, excitedly wagging her tail and saw a big white fluffy cat sitting in Betty and Bill's beautiful blue Jacaranda tree.

'Hello, Daisy May Delaney,' said the fluffy white cat in a very stern voice while flicking her bushy long tail and licking her front paw.

'Hello,' Daisy replied hesitantly. 'Who are you?' she asked slightly confused as she had never seen a cat in her garden before.

'I am Georgina Ann Wagner,' the cat announced in a very confident manner. 'I live with my family next door and I have been watching you for a while from my favourite Jacaranda tree.'

'Oh!' replied a startled Daisy.

'Yes, I know everything about you. Everything!' Georgina the cat continued. 'I have been observing you, Daisy, since the day you arrived and I know your little secret. You don't know how to cuddle!" she exclaimed smugly with her whiskers raised.

Daisy put her head down between her paws feeling very ashamed and embarrassed as she whimpered slightly.

'Oh cheer up, Daisy,' said Georgina. 'You are making this a much bigger problem than it actually is.'

'Am I?' asked Daisy bewildered.

'Yes,' replied the confident cat Georgina, while still flicking her bushy white tail from side to side. 'So what, you cannot cuddle! However, there are many other wonderful things that you can do instead.' The cat continued her conversation as Daisy looked up in amazement.

'Betty and Bill love you just the way you are, Daisy. They love how you fetch the ball with them at the park. They love how you lick their toes while they giggle. They love that you always clean the crumbs off the kitchen floor. They love how you stick your head out the window on your Sunday drives and they especially love that you always smile.'

'Really?' questioned a hopeful Daisy.

'Betty and Bill love you exactly the way you are. They love your big belly, your crooked ears and your droopy eyes. They know that you try so hard to cuddle them, and they know it hurts your feelings each time it doesn't work. They love you just the way you are, and they know you love them and that is all they need.'

'Oh,' replied a surprised Daisy. 'So they still love me even though I cannot cuddle?' Daisy asked the very wise cat. As she waited for a response she looked up to realised Georgina Ann Wagner had disappeared. Puzzled, Daisy searched the back yard for the fascinating fluffy cat. There was no trace of her anywhere.

At sunset Betty and Bill burst in the front door arriving home from working in the big city. 'Daisy, Daisy!' they yelled excitedly. Daisy gleefully ran to them both and licked and licked their faces.

After dinner they all sat together on the fleecy green couch, in front of a warm toasty fire. Daisy was remembering the strange conversation she had earlier with Georgina the cat. It made her feel warm and fuzzy inside, knowing how much Betty and Bill loved her, even though she couldn't cuddle. Then all of a sudden, something very, very strange occurred.

Daisy May Delany somehow found herself moving closer and closer to Betty and Bill. She felt so nice all snuggled on their legs.

"Wow," Daisy thought. The moment she stopped worrying so much about cuddling Betty and Bill, it all just fell into place. It felt wonderful. Daisy discovered she loved being cuddled and she was so comfortable. As Daisy put her head on Betty's lap, she looked out the window through the tartan curtains, and there she was, Georgina Ann Wagner watching and smiling down from her favourite Jacaranda tree.

'Life is simply wonderful,' sighed sleepy Daisy.